The Night Before Thanksgiving

Grosset & Dunlap

Much thanks to Jane O'Connor for inspiring many of the versions in "The Night Before" series, and to my writers group—Mary Nethery, Barbara Kerley Kelly, Ellen Davidson, and Pamela Service—for listening to my stories—some of which are real turkeys. And lastly, this one's for my cousins who had to sit at the kids table. —N. W.

For our family who fills our house with lots of love
and fun on Thanksgiving and especially for Lee
who makes the best darn turkey and mashed potatoes ever! —T.L.

Library of Congress Cataloging-in-Publication Data is available.

ISBN 0-448-42529-7   G H I J

The Night Before Thanksgiving

By Natasha Wing
Illustrated by Tammie Lyon

Grosset & Dunlap, Publishers

'Twas the night before Thanksgiving,
and all through the nation
families got ready
for the big celebration.

At our house my mom baked
three kinds of pies:
pecan and pumpkin,
and apple surprise.

That night we were nestled
all snug in our beds,
while visions of turkey legs
danced in our heads.

The very next morning—
Thanksgiving—yippee!
We got up and watched
the parade on TV!

Relatives arrived from near and far,
by taxi and airplane, by train and by car.

My brother came up
the basement stairs
lugging the kids' table
and folding chairs.

We counted and polished
our best silverware,
then set the two tables
with patience and care.

The turkey went in.
And as more cousins came,
I laughed and I shouted
and called them by name.
"Hi Danny! Hi Donny! Hi Paula and Vickie!
Hi Casey! Hi Cathy! Hi Brenda and Ricky!
Come in from the porch.
Step into the hall.
Now come and play, come and play,
come and play all!"

So up to my room
my cousins they flew.
We played with my toys,
and computer games, too.

We made Pilgrim hats
and funny shoe buckles,
then put on a skit
for aunts and for uncles.

All were assembled
except Uncle Norm,
who called us to say
he was stuck in a storm.

Meanwhile my mother
was getting out yams,
cranberry jelly,
and honey-baked hams.

When Mom wasn't looking
we stuck olives on fingers,
said they were puppets
and grand opera singers.

While dinner was cooking
we played dodgeball outside.
Our tummies were growling,
"Can we eat yet?" we cried.

The timer then sounded!
The turkey was cooked!
Mom opened the oven,
she sniffed, and she looked.
When what to our
watering mouths should appear,
but a marvelous bird
which caused us to cheer.

Its skin—oh so golden!
The drumsticks—so juicy!
The stuffing was fluffy,
thanks to my Aunt Lucy.
Dad slid out the bird.
(It weighed 30 pounds.)
He turned, then he tripped
over one of our hounds.

Up in the air
the turkey did fly!
Over the string beans
and straight for a pie!
My brother and I
made such a clatter,
As we leapt and caught
the bird on a platter.

"All right!" said Grandpa,
"Get on with the carving.
Can't you see that
these people are starving?"

Dad spoke not a word
but went straight to his work.
He sliced up the turkey,
then turned with a jerk.

In front of our house
we heard beeps of a horn,
A trucker delivered
none other than Norm!

With a wink of his eye,
and a twist of his head,
"The party can start!
I made it!" Norm said.

We all took our places,
the food smelled so great,
We started to dig in,
but Dad said to wait.

"We're thankful that everyone
is together this year,
In our home, and our hearts,
where we hold you so dear."

We ate and we ate,
yet last but not least . . .

the very next day
was a leftovers feast!